The Hanukkah Hop!

❄ ❄ GLOSSARY ❄ ❄

bubbe: (Yiddish) grandma

dreidel: (Yiddish) four-sided spinning top used in Hanukkah game. Each side is engraved with a Hebrew letter.

gelt: (Yiddish) money. Small chocolate coins wrapped in gold foil, often used in the give and take of the dreidel game.

latke: (Yiddish) fried potato pancake. Foods fried in oil symbolize the small bit of oil that legend says miraculously kept the eternal flame in the Temple shining for eight days.

Maccabees: family of Jews of the second and first century B.C. who led a small band of rebels in a three-year fight against the army of Syrian-Greek ruler Antiochus IV. Antiochus made practicing the Jewish religion punishable by death. He turned the Temple into a shrine to the Greek gods. The Maccabees' victory led to the rededication of the Temple and a restoration of Jewish political and religious life.

menorah: Jewish lamp or candelabrum, divided into seven or nine branches. The Maccabees relit a seven-branched menorah when they restored the Temple; the nine-branched menorah is used during the celebration of Hanukkah.

nun, gimmel, hei, shin: (Hebrew) the letters on the dreidel, which direct players to give or take pennies, chocolate gelt, or nuts. They also represent the first letter from each word in the sentence, "Nes Gadol Haya Sham," which means "A great miracle happened there."

Temple: the Holy Temple in Jerusalem was the center of Jewish worship in the ancient world.

zayde: (Yiddish) grandpa

To Alexandra—who set this dance in motion . . . —E. S.

For Carmela and Olivia . . . thanks for all of your love and support. Infi infi! —S. D.

SIMON & SCHUSTER BOOKS FOR YOUNG READERS • An imprint of Simon & Schuster Children's Publishing Division • 1230 Avenue of the Americas, New York, New York 10020 • Text copyright © 2011 by Erica Silverman • Illustrations copyright © 2011 by Steven D'Amico • All rights reserved, including the right of reproduction in whole or in part in any form. • SIMON & SCHUSTER BOOKS FOR YOUNG READERS is a trademark of Simon & Schuster, Inc. • For information about special discounts for bulk purchases, please contact Simon & Schuster Special Sales at 1-866-506-1949 or business@simonandschuster.com. • The Simon & Schuster Speakers Bureau can bring authors to your live event. For more information or to book an event, contact the Simon & Schuster Speakers Bureau at 1-866-248-3049 or visit our website at www.simonspeakers.com. • Book design by Chloë Foglia • The text for this book is set in Stempel Schneidler • The illustrations for this book were based on a series of original pencil sketches, digitally rendered on a Mac with Corel Painter 11. Manufactured in India • 0211 MSS

10 9 8 7 6 5 4 3 2 1

first edition

Library of Congress Cataloging-in-Publication Data • Silverman, Erica. • The Hanukkah hop! / Erica Silverman ; • illustrated by Steven D'Amico.—1st ed. • p. cm. • Summary: Rhymed text and illustrations follow a family's activities as they prepare to celebrate Hanukkah. • ISBN 978-1-4424-0604-9 (hardcover) • [1. Stories in rhyme. 2. Hanukkah—Fiction. 3. Jews—United States—Fiction.] I. D'Amico, Steven, ill. II. Title. • PZ8.3.S58425Han 2010 • [E]—dc22 • 2010006064

The Hanukkah Hop!

Written by Erica Silverman
Illustrated by Steven D'Amico

Simon & Schuster Books for Young Readers
NEW YORK   LONDON   TORONTO   SYDNEY

Rachel's twirling streamers.
Daddy blows up blue balloons.
Mommy sizzles latkes as she hums a Hanukkah tune.

Kitzel chases dreidels.
Doodle sneaks a doughnut treat.
Parrot's bob-bob-bobbing
to a jazzy bim-bom beat.

Mommy shines menorahs.
Daddy clears a space to dance.
Rachel swirls with candles
as she sings a bim-bom chant.

"Biddy-biddy bim-bom
bim-bom bop.
I'll whirl all night
at our Hanukkah Hop!"

Bubbes and zaydes zoom in by plane.
Nieces and nephews ride buses and trains.
Great-aunts, second cousins, old friends from afar
are arriving by motorbike, camper, and car.

Rachel opens the front door, swings it wide,
and two-steps all of the guests inside.

"Biddy-biddy bim-bom bim-bom bop.
Come dance at our first ever Hanukkah Hop!"

Gather round menorahs.
Rainbow candles stand in line.
Strike a match and chant the blessing.
Small flames flicker, glow, and shine!

Daddy starts the singing.
Everybody joins along.
Rachel dips and pirouettes
to "Rock of Ages," dreidel song.

"Biddy-biddy bim-bom bim-bom bop.
I flicker like the flames
at our Hanukkah Hop."

Mommy tells the story
of the band of Maccabees—
those ancient freedom fighters
made a stronger army flee.

They restored the ransacked temple.
They relit the altar light
with just a tiny bit of oil
that kept burning for eight nights.

That's why we light the candles
and eat crispy latkes—yum!
"And tonight we dance," adds Rachel,
with a "biddy-biddy bom."

"Biddy-biddy bim-bom
bim-bom bop.
Put your dancing shoes on
for our Hanukkah Hop."

"Who wants to eat?" asks Daddy,
serving platters piled up high
with scrumptious, crunchy latkes,
piping hot and brown and fried.

"Sour cream is best," says Rachel.
"But applesauce is tasty too."

Doodle grabs a jelly doughnut
oozing sweet and drippy goo.

Rachel gazes out the window. She sings, "Biddy-biddy bop.
There are special guests still coming to our Hanukkah Hop."

Time to play with dreidels.
And there's chocolate gelt to win.
Each letter gives direction—

Nun or Gimmel, Hei or Shin:
Give or Take, None or All,
see the dreidels spin and fall.

"I'm a dreidel. Watch!" says Rachel.

She spins. . . .

She stops.

She stares. . . .

DING DONG

The front door opens. . . .
"Yay! Our special guests are here."
And carrying their instruments—
the klezmer band appears!

"Biddy-biddy bim-bom bim-bom bop.
Now we can get stomping
at our Hanukkah Hop!"

Musicians are strumming
and fiddling and drumming.
Singing and chiming,
tooting and humming.

the Mazel-Tones

Cousins are twisting
and jumping and flipping.
Great-aunts and uncles
are stepping and dipping.

Nephews are strutting.
Kitzel is pouncing.
Nieces are swinging.
Doodle's bounce-bouncing.

Bubbes are tapping.
Zaydes are snapping.
Parrot is squawking
with wings flap-flapping.

Toddlers are wiggling and children are giggling.

Daddy is stomping. Mommy is hopping.

Rachel is whirling and bim-bim-bopping.

Biddy-biddy bim-bom bim-bom bop.
Spin! Swing! Sway!

Dive! Jump! Pop!
The party's going wild at the Hanukkah Hop!

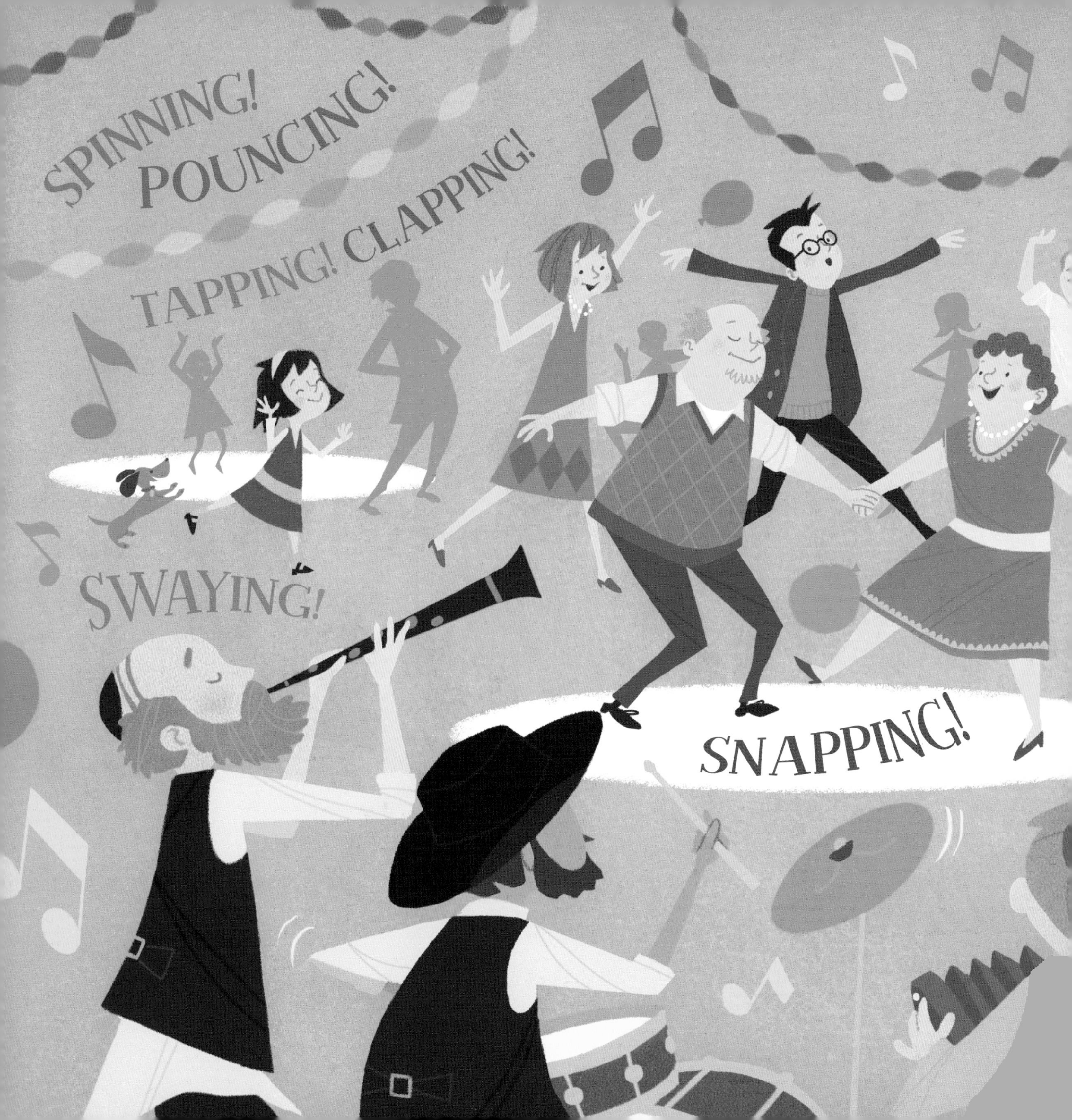
SPINNING!
POUNCING!
TAPPING! CLAPPING!
SWAYING!
SNAPPING!

BOUNCE-BOUNCE-BOUNCING!

WIGGLING, GIGGLING

FLAP-FLAP FLAPPING!

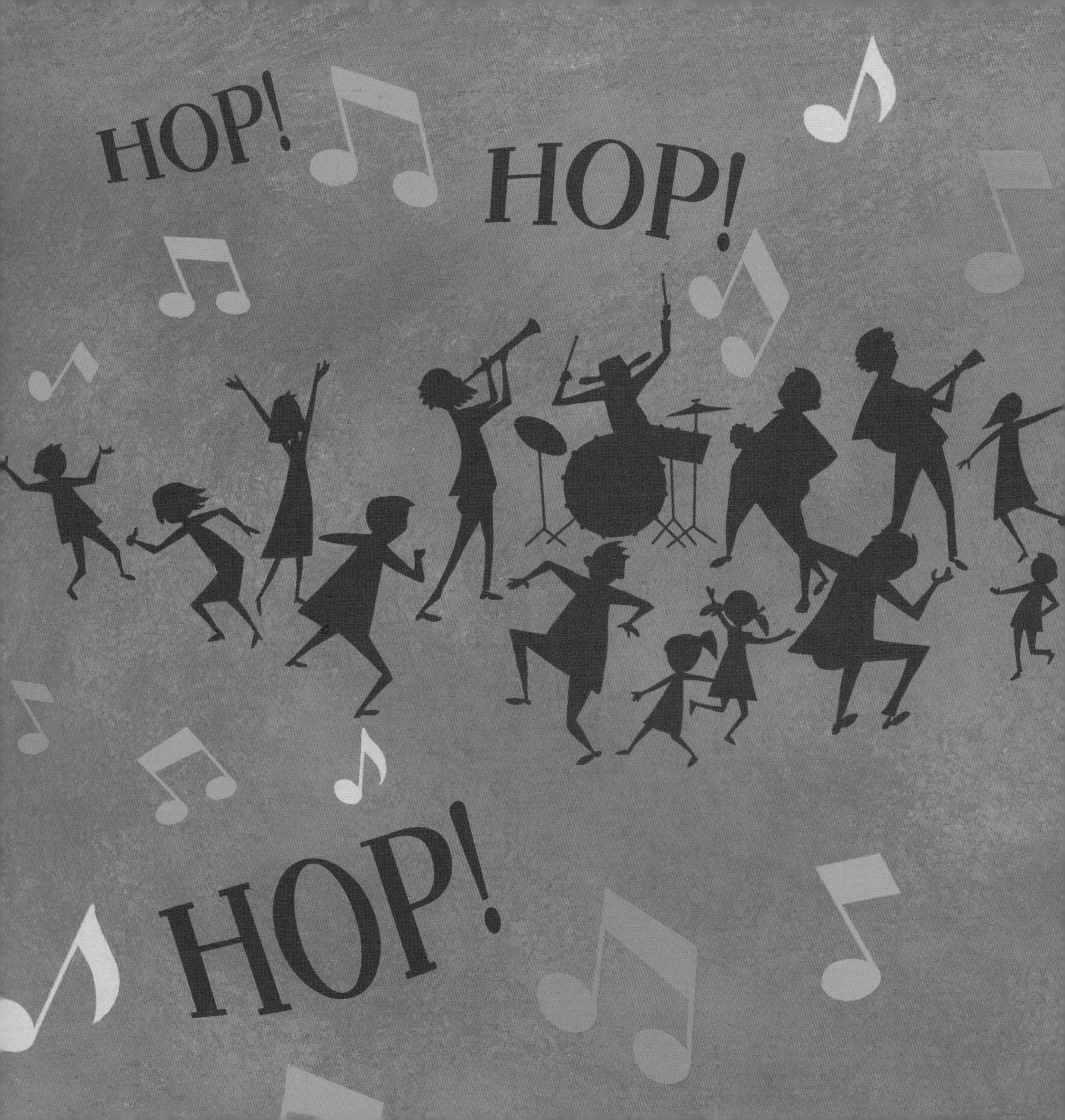

HOP! HOP! HOP!

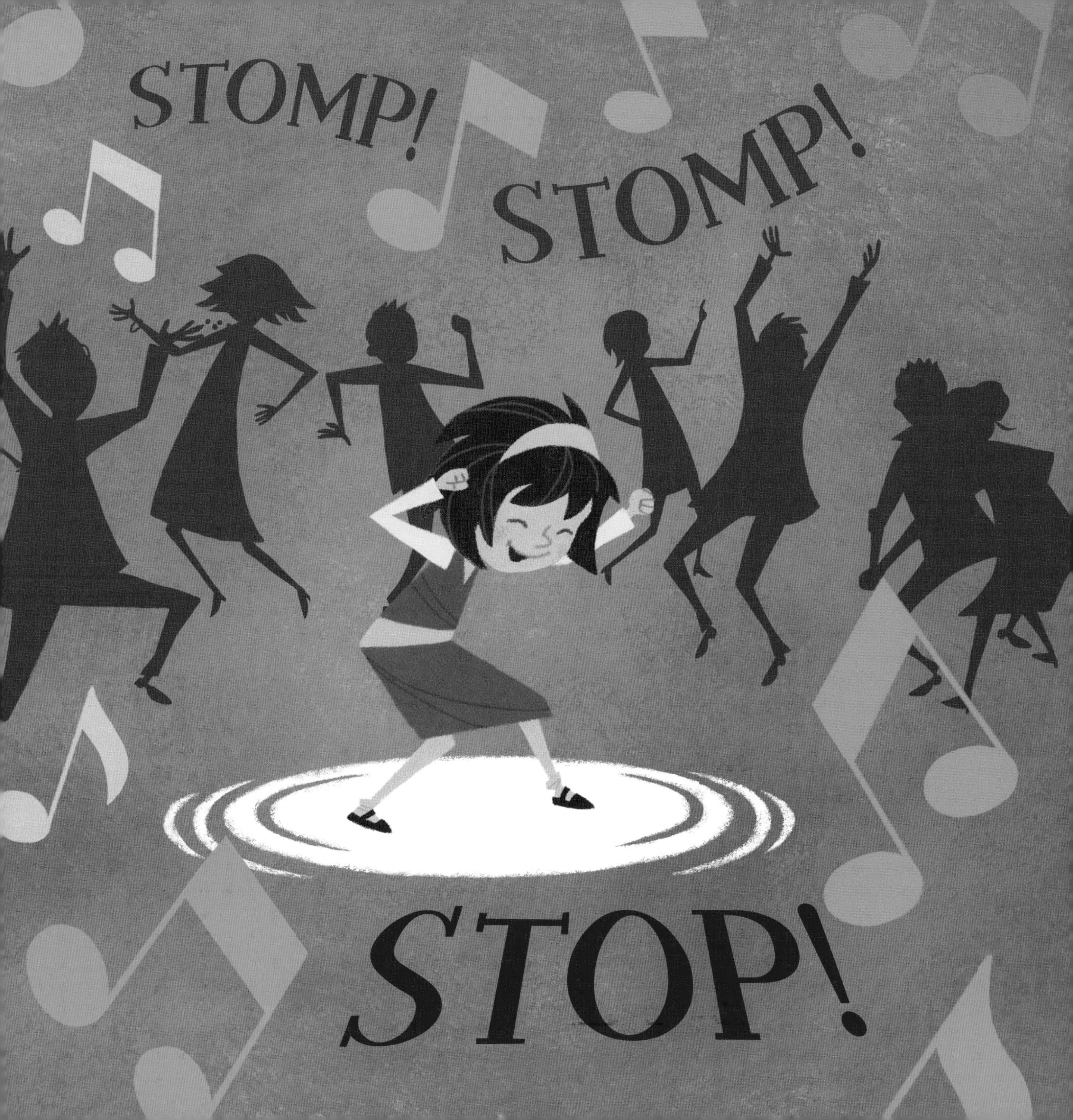

STOMP! STOMP!

STOP!

The klezmer band is drooping.
Their instruments have dropped.

The streamers are falling.
The balloons have all popped.

Daddy's in the kitchen washing dishes and pots.

Mommy brings out blankets
and pillows and cots
for all the snoozing guests
at our Hanukkah Hop.

"Biddy-biddy bim-bom bim-bom bop.
I'm the only one still dancing
at our Hanukkah Hop!"